IGOR THE BIRD WHO COULDN'T SING

In appreciation of the music of
Ornette Coleman

IGOR
THE BIRD WHO COULDN'T SING

STORY & PICTURES BY
SATOSHI KITAMURA

FARRAR STRAUS GIROUX
NEW YORK

Spring had come!
After the long, quiet winter, the time of music had arrived at last.
Igor was thrilled. He knew that spring was the season of songs.
He couldn't wait to sing for the first time in his life.

So when the Dawn Chorus began,

Igor opened his beak wide and joined in. But—

"That was terrible!"
complained one bird.
"Who spoiled our music?" asked another.
"Igor," said a third one.
"He's completely out of tune!"
"Oh," muttered Igor.
"Am I?"

Igor went home and practiced.

He used a metronome and a tuning fork.

He did scales, arpeggios, and études of all sorts.

After a week of hard work, Igor thought he had improved a great deal.

So he went back to his friends
and sang in front of them.
They fell out of the tree laughing.

"Perhaps I need some good music lessons," thought Igor.
He went to see Madam Goose, who was a well-known teacher.
"No problem," said Madam Goose. "Leave it to me.
Singing is easy. Anyone can do it."

"Now, Mr. Igor, listen first
and then sing after me . . .

"*One*, two, three. *One*, two, three.
Keep the beat, Mr. Igor . . .

"Not so fast! Not so loud!
Oh, please, Mr. Igor . . ."

But after a few lessons, Madam Goose started to sing like Igor!
"Mr. Igor," she said with a quaver in her voice, "I have done all I can . . .
I'm sorry. I have failed."

Igor was crestfallen.

"I have no talent!" he thought to himself.

"I love music, but I am a bird who cannot sing.

Oh, how I hate myself."

And he decided never to sing again for as long as he lived.

The problem was
that wherever he went,
there was always someone
singing or enjoying music.

That broke Igor's heart
and left him envious.

He wanted to get away from it all,
but it did not seem so easy . . .

At last, several days later,
he came across an empty plain.
Igor decided to rest his wings
on top of a rock.

It was a quiet place.
Only the winds whispered occasionally.
Igor looked around. "It's rather peaceful here," he thought to himself.
So he collected some twigs and built a nest.

One evening, while sitting in his nest, Igor saw a sunset.
The whole sky glowed scarlet.
It was so beautiful that Igor didn't know whether
he should feel happy or sad.

Suddenly he needed to sing.

He looked around to make sure
there was no one within earshot,
and then he began.

Igor sang and sang.
And as he sang, he felt his music ripple and jolt the evening air.
He felt happy. He felt free.

And then the rock moved . . .

. . . and spoke:

"What wonderful music!"

It wasn't a rock. It was a giant bird.

"But I can't sing," said Igor, amazed.

"On the contrary," exclaimed the bird.

"Your style is unique!

It has woken me up from

a very long sleep.

For the first time in centuries

I want to sing, too.

Please, may I join you?

We'll sing a duet!"

And that was what they did.
Together they sang, filling the sky with their glorious sound.

The music only stopped at daybreak.

"Wasn't that marvelous?" said the giant bird.

"By the way, I'm Dodo. Who, may I ask, are *you*?"

"I'm Igor," said Igor.

"Well, Igor," said Dodo. "Let's form a band! We'll go touring together. We'll play to the world! Come, what do you say?"

"Yes, Dodo, let's do so!" said Igor, and smiled.